W9-CMJ-941

ALL the PLACES WE CALL HOME

For Miracle and Laughter, always.
In memory of my grandmother, Leceita Pryce,
whose bed was so high. — P.G.

To Daddy, who tucked me in with a story
from around the world. — J.M.

ALL the PLACES WE CALL HOME

Written by
Patrice Gopo

Illustrated by
Jenin Mohammed

WORTHY kids™

A Note from the Author

Years ago, in rural Zimbabwe, my oldest daughter took a nap on her great-grandmother's bed. That day I remembered a childhood nap I had once taken on my grandmother's bed in rural Jamaica.

In remembering these experiences, I was struck with the thought that places we have never lived—or no longer live—can deepen our understanding of ourselves. We might even call such places *home*. Or we might use other words. Regardless of what we call these places, they are part of our story. They are part of the story of those we love. And we have the astounding privilege of journeying with the children in our lives as they consider the people *and* places that add to who they are.

ISBN: 978-1-5460-1266-5

WorthyKids, Hachette Book Group, 1290 Avenue of the Americas, New York, NY 10104

Text copyright © 2022 by Patrice Gopo | Art copyright © 2022 by Jenin Mohammed

Library of Congress CIP data

Names: Gopo, Patrice, author. | Mohammed, Jenin, illustrator.
Title: All the places we call home / written by Patrice Gopo ; illustrated by Jenin Mohammed.
Description: First edition. | New York, NY : WorthyKids, [2022] | Audience: Ages 4-8. | Summary: A young girl listens as her mother tells her stories of all the places around the world that their family has called home.
Identifiers: LCCN 2021050512 | ISBN 9781546012665 (hardcover)
Subjects: CYAC: Home—Fiction. | African Americans—Fiction. | Family Life—Fiction. | Families—Fiction.
Classification: LCC PZ7.1.G65457 Al 2022 | DDC [E]--dc23
LC record available at https://lccn.loc.gov/2021050512

Designed by Eve DeGrie

Printed and bound in China · APS

10 9 8 7 6 5 4 3 2 1

At night before I sleep, I twirl my globe.

As the globe slows to a stop, my index finger circles the places that matter to me.

My home in AMERICA.

SOUTH AFRICA

and ZIMBABWE

and JAMAICA too.

"Mama," I say.
"When will we visit?
When will we see?"
"One day, my girl,
one day," Mama answers.

"You'll do more than trace a globe with your finger. You'll travel the world with your feet."

"Tonight, though, can we visit the memories?"

Mama nods.

I climb beneath the covers
with Pink Blanket, ready for sleep.
"Where are we?" Mama asks.

"America," I say.

Where I watch morning sun slide through my window. Where I draw pictures of my family. Where I sink into my pillow, close my eyes, and dream.

"And where shall we go?"

"**South Africa.** Where I was born."

My answer summons Mama's stories, stories
that send us soaring back in time to when I was
a baby. Out my window. Down my street.
Across water. Across continents.
To the shadow of Table Mountain.
To a bedroom in a bustling city.

Mama tells me about my first night in my first home:
the rumbling road close by, the amber balls of lamplight,
the hint of ocean salt in the breeze.
I snuggled against her chest,
my body in the world
of deep baby sleep.

"Did I wake up?"
Mama laughs, "Only when I put you in your bassinet."
Then she would reach for me and return me to my dreams.

"Where shall we go now?"
Mama asks.

"Zimbabwe," I say, "To Gogo's home."

Again, Mama's stories take us far from my bed. Across land. Across borders. To my great-grandmother's home in rural Zimbabwe.

Mama tells me about a day
when the air was warm like a breath in our
cupped hands. Outside, a dense fog hid
the lush hills and msasa trees. The call
of a rooster joined the rustle of leaves. Inside, I
slept in Mama's arms, curved into her side.

"Did I stay in your arms?" I ask.
Mama shakes her head. "I placed you
on Gogo's bed."
    That day I drifted toward sleep in my
daddy's grandmother's home,
mist wetting the window,
gray light piercing
the dim room.

"Where shall we go now?"
Mama asks once more.

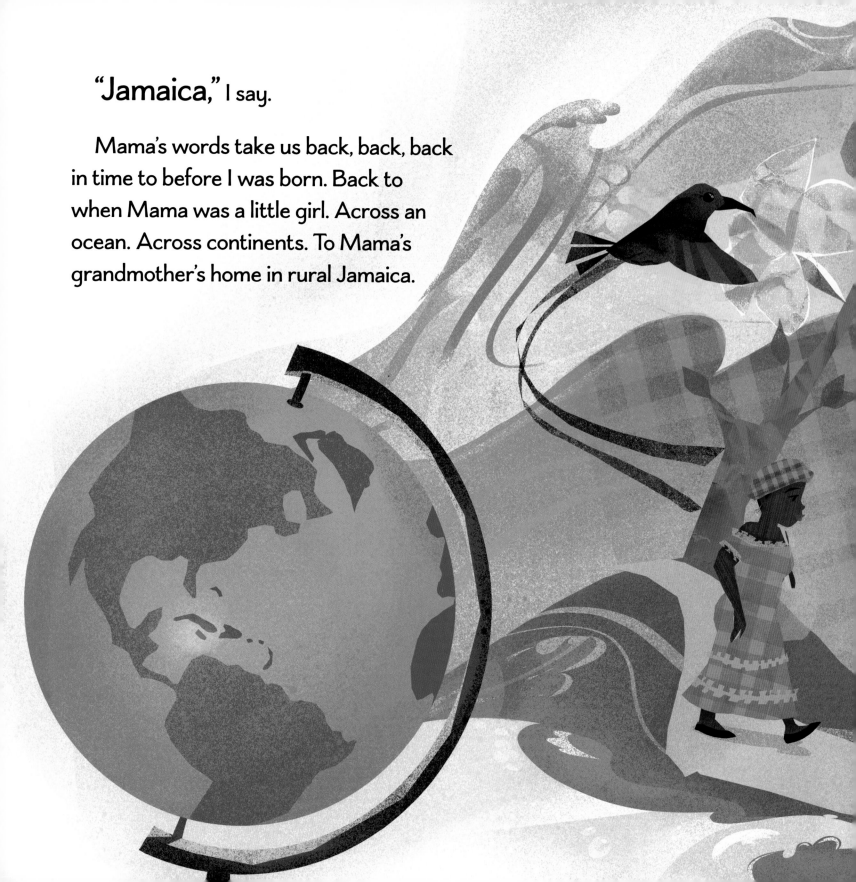

"Jamaica," I say.

Mama's words take us back, back, back in time to before I was born. Back to when Mama was a little girl. Across an ocean. Across continents. To Mama's grandmother's home in rural Jamaica.

Mama says back then
she looked up to a high bed,
her grandmother's bed.

There was light from the window, the small window just above where the bed met the wall. The afternoon sun parted the shadows with streaks of gold.

"How did you climb into the bed?" I ask.
"My mama lifted me." Mama remembers
drifting toward sleep, the fragrant scent of
tropical flowers saturating the air
and a symphony of songbirds
warbling in the trees.

"Where shall we go now?"
Mama asks me one last time.

"Where we live."

"South Africa. Zimbabwe. Jamaica. Come with me."
South Africa swirls through my thinking.
Zimbabwe blooms in my imagination.
Jamaica sprouts wings.

We travel back.

Across lands. Across borders.
Back to my bedroom.

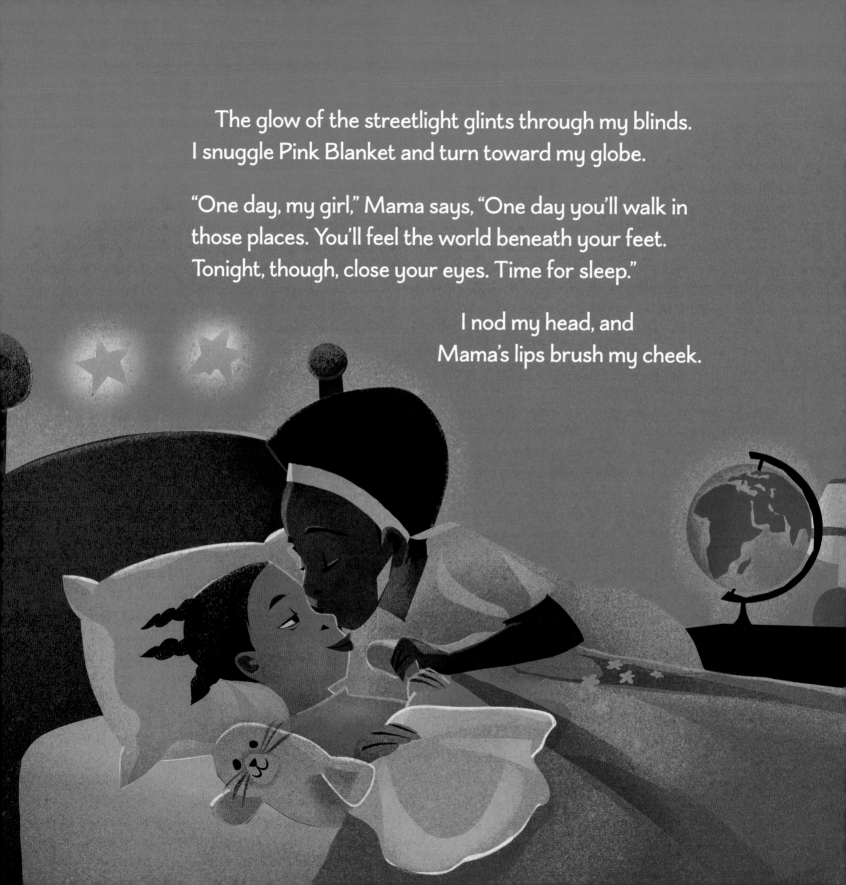

The glow of the streetlight glints through my blinds.
I snuggle Pink Blanket and turn toward my globe.

"One day, my girl," Mama says, "One day you'll walk in
those places. You'll feel the world beneath your feet.
Tonight, though, close your eyes. Time for sleep."

I nod my head, and
Mama's lips brush my cheek.

Here I'll sleep. And here I'll dream
of these places that matter to me.